This book is dedicated to
the real Hannah Stone
whose McCurdy descendants
live at Morgan Farm today.

HANNAH'S FARM

The Seasons on an Early American Homestead

written and illustrated with wood engravings by

MICHAEL McCURDY

HOLIDAY HOUSE/NEW YORK

Morgan Farm nestles against Warner Mountain in the
Berkshire Hills. In winter snow covers the floor of the forest
and fields. It covers Lake Buel Road—and it nearly covers
the small barn next to the house where Big Dan the horse
lives and Bertha the cow makes milk and where the chickens
cackle and huddle close together for warmth.

Winter is a quiet time, mostly spent indoors. In the kitchen, Mother Stone cooks Sunday dinner in the pot above the fire. Father Stone brings in wood from the shed and milk from Bertha. Grandpa Morgan sits in his rocking chair and tells the stories of his youth, when he cleared the forest to build Morgan Farm. Grandma Morgan cleans house and keeps her eye on Grandpa, while little Tobias Stone plays on the kitchen floor. Hannah Stone looks out the frost-covered windows. "How much longer will it be until spring comes?" she asks.

Hannah sits every morning with Mother and studies her lessons. She taps her foot and looks at the door. "When can I go help Grandpa and Father in the woods?" she asks. "First things first, Hannah," Mother tells her. But one day Father and Grandpa ask Hannah to go with them to cut trees for next winter's firewood. Tobias can't come—he's too little. Father uses a sled pulled by the family's two oxen, Jeb and Seth. Wood has to be cut now when the trees can be dragged easily and when the sap can't slow down the saw blade. "Besides, there are no mosquitoes at this time of year," says Father. Hannah learns all about trees. She knows which ones to cut and which ones burn best. It is quiet in the woods except for the sound of Father and Grandpa's two-man saw cutting back and forth, back and forth.

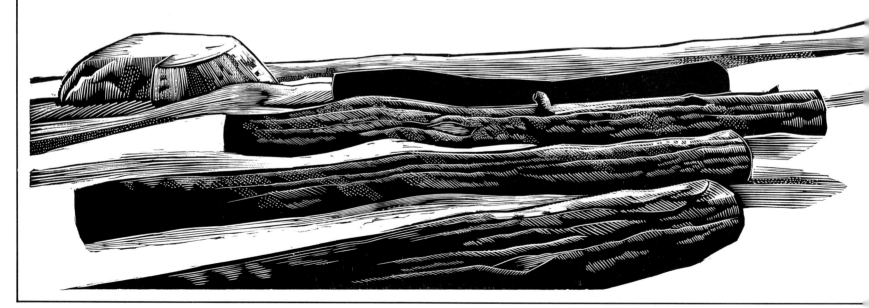

When early spring comes, Hannah helps Father and Grandpa tap sugar maple trees. The tree's sap drips slowly into the wooden buckets fastened to the trees. When they are nearly full, Hannah pours the sap into a much bigger bucket on the sled. Jeb pulls it to the family's maple syrup shed near the woods. Grandma is waiting to boil down the sap to make maple syrup. It is sugaring-off time, and Hannah and Tobias are given a little syrup on a handful of snow, one of the few sweets they ever get to have. "You can eat as much as you want," Grandma says, "but be careful you don't get sick to your stomach!"

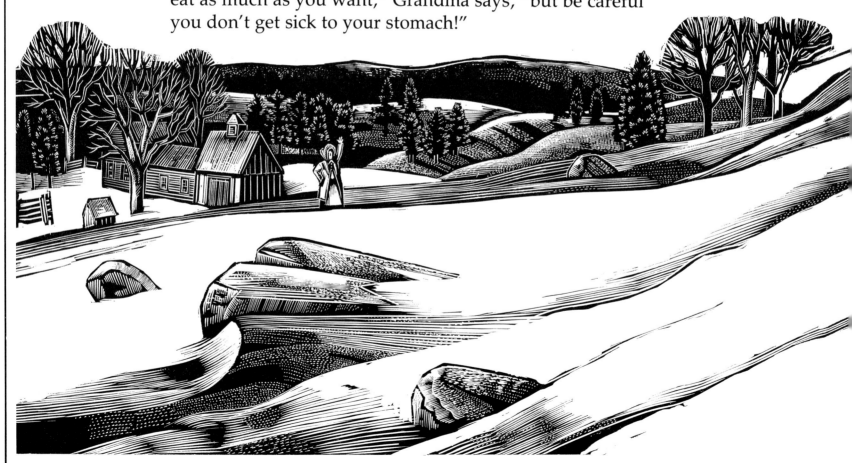

When it is warmer, the neighboring men arrive in their wagons. They all have sharp axes and saws. "Hello!" they shout to Hannah and Tobias. They start cutting down trees for the new barn. Some workers take stones from the clearing while others use them to build a foundation. With tools called an adz and a broadax, the men hew a fallen tree, making a square beam which will be placed on top of the stone foundation. More beams will be cut like this for the frame. Hannah and Tobias help by taking water buckets to the thirsty men. Mother and Grandma hurry out into the yard and set up a table with cider jugs and food. "There's enough food here to feed an army," says Grandma. "Good," says Mother, "I reckon the men will be hungry."

The men have come and gone for several days now. The barn's frame is up, and the men are going to split the rest of the trees into planks. They use wedges and hammers with funny names such as "gluts" and "beetles." It's very hard work, but Grandma always says, "Many hands make lightsome work!" Once the planks have been cut the neighbors leave, and Grandpa and Father do the rest of the work themselves. They nail the boards to the barn's frame. They know that fresh wood will shrink, but they don't worry, because it will make cracks in the barn which will help air circulate around the hay. Hannah loves the smell of the cut wood, and Tobias finds special hiding places in the barn. "This barn is going to be a wonderful place to play on rainy days!" Hannah tells her little brother. Tobias thinks so too.

While Father and Grandpa finish the big barn, Hannah has to help Mother plant corn. Mother hitches Big Dan to the plow, and Hannah walks behind, dropping corn kernels into the furrows. Tobias follows Hannah and makes certain

each kernel is buried under the soil. "It's hot work," says Hannah. "I wish I could help Grandma instead." Grandma is cooler in the garden where she's planting most of the food the family will eat during the summer and following winter.

By June Grandma's garden is almost full-grown and the ryegrass in the hayfield is high. Father and Grandpa cut the grass with their scythes. Everybody in the family gathers it together into rows so that once it is dry it can be pitched into the wagon. Hannah piles the hay as Father and Grandpa throw it up to her. Tobias sits up front with Grandma, who steers Big Dan. The hay will be stored in the new barn. Before the barn was built, Father stored it in a hole in the ground! "The cows will have plenty of hay to eat all next winter," Hannah tells everyone.

On the Fourth of July, Independence Day, everybody stops farm work and prepares for an afternoon of picnicking. Hannah's parents invite all the neighbors to share the event. The guests bring food for the harvest table behind the farmhouse. Hannah eats so much she bursts a seam in her calico dress. Mr. Forrester falls asleep under the big oak tree near the new barn and snores too loudly. Mr. Kenning tunes his fiddle and plays a lively jig, but nobody dances because everyone has eaten too much! Old Mrs. Bent tells stories to Hannah and Tobias about what family life was like when she was a young girl and Indians roamed the Berkshire Hills near Great Barrington. Mr. Van Fleet smokes his clay pipe and dreams about how many pigs he'll be taking to market this year. "Listen," cries Tobias. "I can hear bells ringing and cannon shots from town."

It is August now and the beginning of harvesttime, what Grandpa Morgan calls Lammas Day. "The Great Harvest Fly," the cicada, is singing in the nearby trees. Hannah helps bring in the melons, potatoes, beets, and onions. She puts them in the root cellar beneath the house, where they stay just the right temperature in hot or cold weather. Hannah and Tobias hide in the root cellar when the weather gets too hot.

By autumn the grain has been threshed, the hay is in the new barn, and the corn has been picked. Father has built a crib for storing the corn, which he will feed to his new pigs. Hannah's summer chores are over, but now it is time to pick apples and make apple cider. "This is my favorite time of year," Hannah announces to the family. "I want to be the first to taste the new cider!"

"Then you'll have to work hard picking apples," Father replies.

In October Father comes home one day with Mr. Ogden. "Children, Mr. Ogden is going to help us harvest our apples," Father says. Grandpa brings out the tall ladders and the picking begins. Father and Mr. Ogden pick the eating apples very carefully so as not to bruise them. The reddest and the shiniest will be saved for Christmas. Hannah and Mother store all the best apples in straw-packed boxes and put them in the cellar. Grandma picks other apples for drying. "Will you use them to make your special apple pies?" Hannah asks. Hannah and Tobias pick the poorest apples to be used for Grandma's applesauce and vinegar.

The days are growing shorter, and Hannah has to bundle up in her wool clothing to keep warm. New snow has fallen, but Father is glad because it is easier to travel in the family's horse-drawn sleigh. Grandma and Mother have hung many apple slices along the ceiling for drying. Hannah and Tobias have gathered nuts, and the root cellar is full. There are new cows in the barn, and they are making milk and eating the

fresh hay from summer. Hannah looks forward to Christmas at Morgan Farm. Mother and Grandma busy themselves cooking the big dinner the family will eat on Christmas Day. The fire is burning in the fireplace, the candles are lit, and Hannah and Tobias are snug in bed in the loft, thinking of Christmas. The sweet smell of Grandma's apple pie is all she remembers until morning.

Christmas Day! Father and Grandpa have been up very early attending to farm chores. Mother and Grandma finish cooking the Christmas dinner. It will be the biggest dinner yet! Mr. Ogden and Mr. Van Fleet have been invited. Mr. Ogden is going to bring a fig layer cake. Hannah and Tobias see the Christmas tree on the table, reaching to the ceiling. The tree is a new addition to the Morgan Christmas. Grandma is skeptical. "In my day we left trees in the forest, where they belong!" she says as she bastes the Christmas goose.

By early afternoon everyone sits down to eat. The table groans under the weight of food: there is roast goose and venison, baked squash, mashed turnips, carrots, parsley, onions, apple pie, mince pie, nuts, suet puddings, fruit drops, barley sugar rings, and apple cider. There is also Father's famous eggnog. Mr. Van Fleet surprises everyone by giving two small tin horns to Hannah and Tobias. "You see, where I come from in Holland, Christmas gifts are given to all the little children," he explains.

"What a wonderful idea," says Hannah. Then she and Tobias blow their horns at the table while everybody gives a cheer to Father Christmas!

Library of Congress Cataloging-in-Publication Data

McCurdy, Michael. A42-

Hannah's farm : the seasons on an early American homestead /
written and illustrated by Michael McCurdy.—1st ed.
p.   cm.
Summary: As the seasons roll by, all the members of Hannah's
family, Grandma, Grandpa, Father, Mother, and little Tobias, engage
in activities on their farm in the Berkshire Hills of Massachusetts.
[1. Farm life—Fiction.   2. Seasons—Fiction.]   I. Title.
PZ7.M4784163Han   1988
[E]—dc19   87-29631   CIP   AC
ISBN 0-8234-0700-4